Please visit our website, www.garethstevens.com. For a free color catalog of all our high-quality books, call toll free 1-800-542-2595 or fax 1-877-542-2596.

Cataloging-in-Publication Data

Names: Claybourne, Anna.
Title: Mysterious experiments / Anna Claybourne.
Description: New York : Gareth Stevens Publishing, 2019. | Series: Ultimate science lab | Includes glossary and index.
Identifiers: ISBN 9781538235386 (pbk.) | ISBN 9781538235409 (library bound) | ISBN 9781538235393 (6pack)
Subjects: LCSH: Science--Experiments--Juvenile literature.
Classification: LCC Q164.C5725 2019 | DDC 507.8--dc23

First Edition

Published in 2019 by
Gareth Stevens Publishing
111 East 14th Street, Suite 349
New York, NY 10003

Author: Anna Claybourne
Science consultant: Thomas Canavan
Experiment illustrations: Jessica Secheret
Other illustrations: Richard Watson
Photos: Shutterstock
Design: Supriya Sahai, with Emma Randall
Editor: Joe Fullman, with Julia Adams

Printed in the United States of America

CPSIA compliance information: Batch #CW19GS: For further information contact Gareth Stevens, New York, New York at 1-800-542-2595.

CONTENTS

START EXPERIMENTING!

This book is packed with exciting experiments that make objects disappear, cause food to glow in the dark, or are so incredible you won't believe your eyes! But there's nothing magical in these pages—it's all real-life amazing SCIENCE.

BE ECO-FRIENDLY!

First things first. As scientists, we aim to be as environmentally friendly as possible. Experiments require lots of different materials, including plastic ones, so we need to make sure we reuse and recycle as much as we can ...

* Some experiments use plastic straws; rather than buying a large amount, ask in coffee shops or restaurants whether they can spare a few for your experiments.

* Old cereal boxes are great for experiments that use cardboard.

* Save old school worksheets and other paper you no longer need, to reuse for experiments.

WHAT YOU'LL NEED

You can do most of these experiments with everyday items you'll find around the house.

Some useful things to have handy are ...

* Paper and cardboard

* Pens and pencils

* String

* Glue

* Tape

* Straws (plastic ones are best)

* Plates, bowls, jugs, and plastic food containers

* Scissors

* Rubber bands

* Paper cups

* Balloons

STAY SAFE!

Experiments are fun, but some of them can be dangerous if they're not done carefully … so don't forget these safety tips:

✱ You will need an adult to help with experiments that involve cooking and heating, matches and candles, and sharp cutting tools. Wherever an experiment has something like this in it, you'll see this sign to remind you:

⚠ ASK AN ADULT!

✱ Follow all the instructions carefully to make sure you use all the equipment and materials in a safe way.

✱ If an experiment requires you to stand on a chair, make sure you have someone to assist you. Check that the chair is placed in a stable position and ask the person helping you to hold the chair while you are using it.

✳ Stand back from anything that's moving fast, or that involves eruptions or explosions. And don't throw, shoot, or whirl things around unless you're completely sure there's no one nearby.

And remember...

Always do experiments somewhere that's easy to clean up, like a kitchen or bathroom—NOT on the fancy carpet! And make sure you do clean up after yourself. Some of these experiments are messy!

So, are you ready to see some science? Step this way ...

MYSTERIOUS EXPERIMENTS

Science can behave in some VERY strange ways. This book is full of experiments that make you go "Wow! How does that work!?" and "Wait—WHAT just happened!?" They're great for amazing your friends and family.

WHY IS SCIENCE SURPRISING?
Most of the time, our brains make good predictions about how objects and materials will behave, based on our past experiences. However, sometimes an experiment can make something behave in an unexpected way—it might even seem impossible! It's breaking the rules our brains have learned, but it's not breaking the rules of science. That's what will make you gasp!

Mysterious science

None of these things are magical—they all happen according to the rules of science. But the more you learn about science, the more you find out that it really IS quite bizarre. For instance, did you know that ...

A particle (tiny bit of matter) can actually be in two places at once.

Time can slow down if you're moving fast enough!

At very low temperatures, helium can flow against gravity.

Mobius madness

Let the weirdness begin with this fun mini experiment!

You need a strip of thin cardboard, about 1 inch (2.5 cm) wide and 12 inches (30 cm) long. Bring the ends together to make a loop, but before joining them together, flip one end over so that there's a twist in the strip. Then tape the ends together. The twisted strip is called a Mobius strip.

Take a pair of scissors with a pointy tip, and cut into the middle of the strip. Ask an adult to help if it's tricky.
Cut all the way along the middle until you get back to where you started.

You've cut the strip in half, right ...

HOW DOES IT WORK?

When you twist the end over, you join one edge of the strip to the other edge. Instead of two edges, it now has one long continuous edge. You can't cut it in two because one side is continuous with the other. Simple, isn't it?

... OR HAVE YOU???

9

AMAZIN' RAISIN

What do you mean, you've never dropped a raisin into your soda? You just have to try it! There's mysterious science at work.

WHAT YOU'LL NEED:
* A new bottle of colorless soda (such as Sprite® or 7 Up®)
* A tall, clear glass
* Raisins

This will work with most sodas, but clear ones make it easier for you to see what the raisins are up to.

1. Open the bottle and pour soda into the glass, filling it almost to the top. Wait for the bubbles to settle down (don't shake the bottle first!).

2. Take a few raisins (large ones works best) and gently drop them into the glass. Watch what they do. Give it a few minutes—it may take a little while to see what's happening.

3. If it works, your raisins will start to behave strangely. They'll sink to the bottom, wait there for a bit, then float up to the surface. After hanging around there for a while, they'll head back to the bottom—and repeat!

HOW DOES IT WORK?

The soda has carbon dioxide gas dissolved in it—this is what makes the bubbles. The rough, crinkly surface of the raisins helps carbon dioxide bubbles come out of the liquid and stick to the raisins. When a raisin has enough bubbles stuck to it, they make it lighter, and up it floats. But when it reaches the surface, some of the bubbles pop. The raisin is now heavier again, and sinks. And so on …

You can try this with other objects, too. What happens if you use a berry, a jelly bean, or a bit of chocolate instead of a raisin? What works best?

SUGAR LIGHTS

Where does light come from? The sun, the stars, light bulbs, flashlights, candles, and glow sticks, of course. You've probably heard of fireflies and deep-sea fish that can light up, too. Oh, and sugar lumps!

WHAT YOU'LL NEED:

* Sugar lumps
* Hard, sugary candies, such as mints
* A plastic sandwich bag (self-sealing if possible)
* Pliers
* A very dark place

(!) ASK AN ADULT!

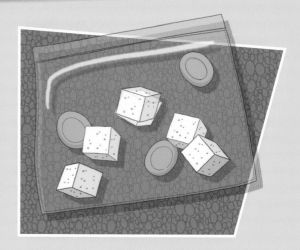

1. Put a few sugar lumps and candies into the sandwich bag, and seal it up or tie it closed. This is to make sure you don't spill sugar everywhere.

2. Go into your dark place. It could be a dark room at night, or just make a dark den under a blanket.

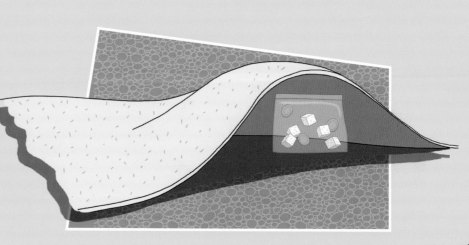

3. Ask an adult to use the pliers, as they can nip your fingers. In the dark, get the adult to hold the pliers around a candy or sugar lump (through the bag, with the sugar and candies inside).

4. Watch carefully as the adult squeezes the pliers to crush the candy or sugar lump as fast as possible. If it's dark enough, you should see a glow of light.

HOW DOES IT WORK?
This strange light is called triboluminescence. It's made by some materials when they are crushed, squeezed, or ripped apart. Scientists aren't really sure why!

There are more ways to make triboluminescence. **TRY THESE!**

▪ Rip open a self-seal envelope.
▪ Stick two strips of clear tape or packing tape together, then rip them apart as fast as possible.
▪ Get two rose quartz crystals and rub them together.
▪ Ask an adult to put some sugar lumps in a food processor, and blend them.

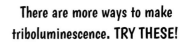

THE BOUNCY EGG

Take a perfectly normal, raw egg, and turn it into a bouncy rubber ball (well, an egg-shaped ball!) with this bizarre experiment.

WHAT YOU'LL NEED:

* A raw egg
* White vinegar
* A small jar or food container (big enough for the egg) with a lid
* A larger container or bowl
* A plate

The large container is to catch any vinegar that may leak out, as it's pretty smelly.

1. Take your egg and gently put it into the small container. Pour in white vinegar until it completely covers the egg. Put the lid on and press or screw it down firmly.

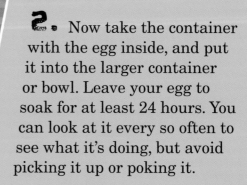

2. Now take the container with the egg inside, and put it into the larger container or bowl. Leave your egg to soak for at least 24 hours. You can look at it every so often to see what it's doing, but avoid picking it up or poking it.

HOW DOES IT WORK?

An egg's shell contains a material called calcium carbonate, which makes it hard. Vinegar reacts with calcium carbonate and makes it dissolve away, leaving the inner part, which is a stretchy skin or "membrane." It can still hold the raw egg in, though it's not as strong— and it can bounce.

3. When the time is up, take off the lid and carefully take the egg out. It will have strange bits of "skin" on it—gently wash them off under a tap.

4. The egg should feel strangely soft and rubbery. Drop it onto the plate from a few inches up in the air, and it should bounce!

Do this really carefully, as the egg inside is still raw, and it may splat open. The person who splats it has to clean it up!

THE VANISHING GLASS

Want to know how to make a normal, everyday drinking glass disappear before your very eyes? Amaze your friends or parents with some mysterious science magic!

WHAT YOU'LL NEED:

* A small, plain, clear drinking glass
* A clear mixing bowl, big enough for the glass to fit right inside
* A large bottle of sunflower oil (the kind used for cooking)

1. Make sure the glass and the bowl are clean and dry. Stand the glass inside the bowl.

2. Pour some oil into the bowl, so that it comes halfway up the glass. Pour some into the glass, too, so that it comes up to the same level.

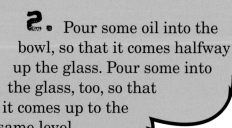

If it doesn't work very well, try another glass. There are different types of glass, so some might match the oil better than others.

3. Look through the side of the bowl. What's happened to the bottom of the glass? If your experiment is working, it will have vanished!

4. Keep pouring more oil into the bowl, until the glass is completely submerged. Ta-daaa—it disappears!

HOW DOES IT WORK?

Glass is see-through, but you can still see it, can't you? That's because of the way light bends, or "refracts," when it shines through different materials. When you look at a glass, you can see the edges because the refraction makes you see darker and lighter areas in the glass. However, the amount of refraction that happens in oil is roughly the same as for glass. So when the oil surrounds the glass, light passes straight through the glass, and you can't see it!

THE MIGHTY STRAW

Try to stick a straw into a potato and you'll have trouble. Or your friends will — you won't, because you know the secret! In fact, you might be able to stick it all the way through ...

WHAT YOU'LL NEED:
* A medium-sized raw potato
* Plastic drinking straws

Bendy straws won't work for this experiment. If you only have bendy straws, cut the ends off neatly, just below the bendy part.

1. First, try to stick a straw into a potato. It has to be a raw one—no cheating with cooked potatoes! It's very difficult, because the potato is hard and the straw bends and crumples.

2. To make it work, you have to hold the straw in your fist, and put your thumb over the open end, like this. Don't squeeze it too hard, but hold it firmly.

3. Hold the potato in the other hand, but don't have your hand right underneath it. If the straw goes all the way through, you don't want it to stick into your hand as well!

4. Now lift up the hand holding the straw, and quickly and firmly jab it into the potato. You'll be amazed to find it really does go right in!

HOW DOES IT WORK?

It's all about the air inside the straw. When you don't have your thumb over the end, the straw is quite weak, as it only has thin walls, and crumples easily. But with your thumb over the end, the air in the straw gets stuck inside. It makes the straw stiffer and stronger, so it works more like a strong, solid stick.

BLAST THAT BALL

If you blast a ball with a blow dryer, it will fly away across the room, won't it? Nope! Try this experiment — and prepare to be blown away!

WHAT YOU'LL NEED:

* A blow dryer (with a "cool" setting)
* A table tennis ball
* A tube from the inside of a paper towel roll

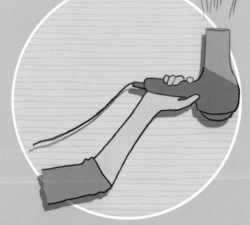

1. Turn the blow dryer on to its "cool" setting, and tilt it so the air is blasting upward. Carefully place the table tennis ball in the jet of air around 12 inches (30 cm) above the dryer. It should stay hanging in the air.

2. If you carefully tilt the blow dryer, the ball should stay suspended in the air even though it's no longer directly above the dryer.

See what other lightweight objects you can keep in the air using the dryer. Try pieces of newspaper. What's the biggest piece you can keep airborne?

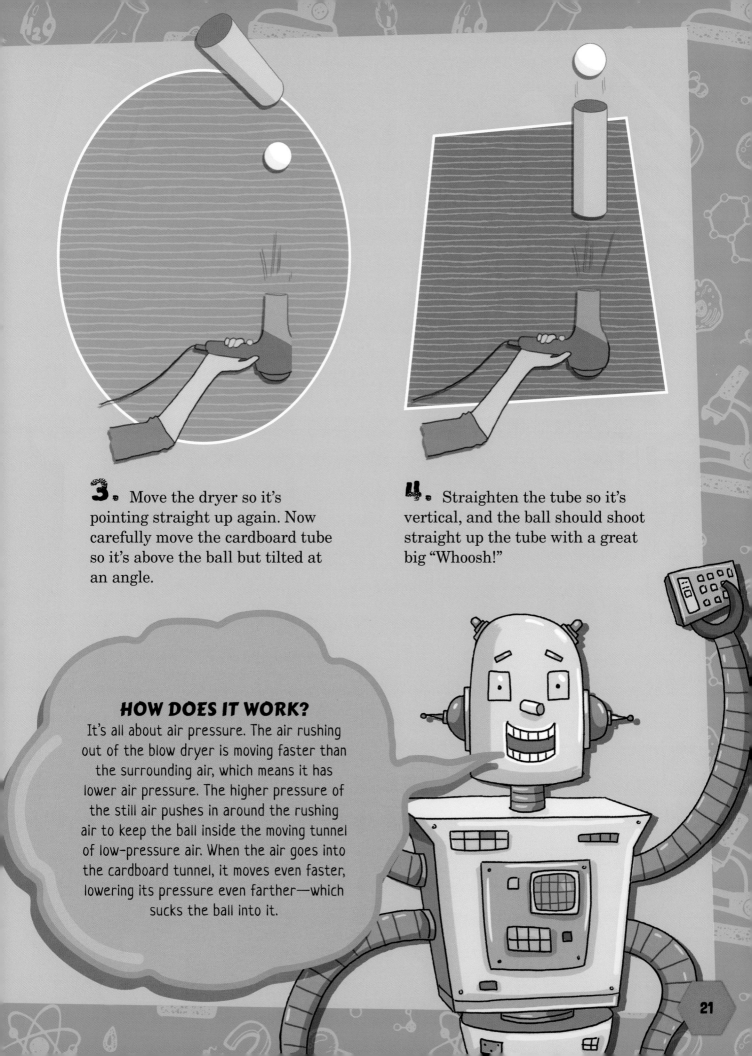

3. Move the dryer so it's pointing straight up again. Now carefully move the cardboard tube so it's above the ball but tilted at an angle.

4. Straighten the tube so it's vertical, and the ball should shoot straight up the tube with a great big "Whoosh!"

HOW DOES IT WORK?

It's all about air pressure. The air rushing out of the blow dryer is moving faster than the surrounding air, which means it has lower air pressure. The higher pressure of the still air pushes in around the rushing air to keep the ball inside the moving tunnel of low-pressure air. When the air goes into the cardboard tunnel, it moves even faster, lowering its pressure even farther—which sucks the ball into it.

FLOWERS AND STARS

Make the flowers bloom and the stars come out with this wonderfully simple paper experiment. All you need to make it work is water.

WHAT YOU'LL NEED:

* Paper
* Colored pencils or crayons
* Scissors
* A large, shallow plate or container

1. Draw flower and star shapes on the paper. They should each have a circle in the middle, and petals or points around the edge, like these ones.

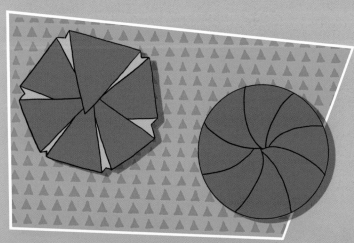

2. Cut out your flower and star shapes, and, if you like, decorate and color them in. Then fold all the petals or points inward, so that they cover the middle.

3. Put your container or plate on a flat surface, and fill it with water almost to the top. Now drop your stars and flowers in, folded side upward.

You can take the flowers and stars out, leave them to dry, and use them over and over again.

HOW DOES IT WORK?

Paper is a porous substance, which means it is full of tiny spaces that can soak up water. As water soaks into the paper, it makes it swell and get thicker. When the paper is thicker, it's hard for the folds to stay shut, and they quickly get pushed open.

For a fancier version, make one larger star or flower, and one smaller one. Stick the smaller one inside the bigger one, and fold them both up. The larger, outside one will open first, and the inside one will open more slowly, as it takes longer for the water to reach it.

EGG IN A BOTTLE

This experiment is great for amazing a crowd of people. They'll get to see an egg being sucked right inside a glass bottle by the sheer power of science.

WHAT YOU'LL NEED:

* A glass bottle with a wide opening, about 1½ inches (4 cm) across
* An egg that's just slightly wider than the opening of your bottle
* A pan
* A stove
* A sink
* Cooking oil
* Matches

⚠ ASK AN ADULT!

1. Ask an adult to hard-boil your egg by boiling it in a pan of water for 10 minutes, then cool it in cold water. When it's cool, carefully peel off the shell, and rinse the egg.

The type of wide-topped bottle you need is sometimes used for juice, iced tea, or salsa. An old-fashioned glass milk bottle will also work well.

2. Make sure your glass bottle is clean and dry. Use your finger to smear a little cooking oil around the neck and top of the bottle.

3. Sit the egg in the top of the bottle to check that it is too big to fall in. Then put it to one side, within easy reach. (If it does fall in, take it out and try again with a larger egg.)

For the egg, if you get a "mixed sizes" box of eggs, you should find one that's just right.

4. Ask an adult to light a match, wait a second or two, then drop it into the bottle. Quickly put the egg on top of the bottle, and it should start being pulled down inside.

5. It should take just a couple of seconds for the egg to be completely sucked inside the bottle.

HOW DOES IT WORK?

Air expands as it gets hotter, and shrinks as it gets cooler. The flame heats up the air in the bottle making it expand. With the egg on top, the match goes out, and the air starts to cool and shrink, reducing the pressure in the bottle. The air pressure on the outside is higher, so it pushes down on the egg, and forces it inside.

INVISIBLE SNUFFER

With this experiment, you can put out a candle flame without touching it or blowing it. Instead, it gets snuffed out by a mysterious stream of something invisible!

WHAT YOU'LL NEED:

* A small pitcher
* White vinegar
* Baking soda (sometimes known as bicarbonate of soda)
* A teaspoon
* A candle, holder, and matches

⚠ ASK AN ADULT!

1. First, ask an adult to put the candle in its holder, and light it with a match. Stand it somewhere safe, and put the pitcher near it, but not too close—about 12 inches (30 cm) away.

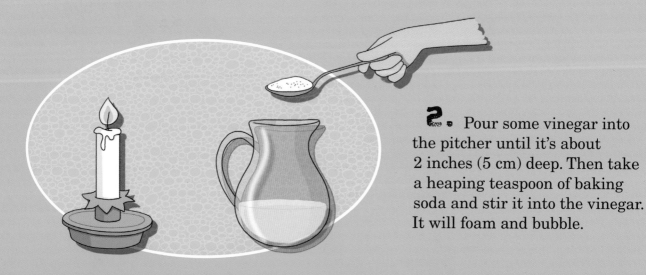

2. Pour some vinegar into the pitcher until it's about 2 inches (5 cm) deep. Then take a heaping teaspoon of baking soda and stir it into the vinegar. It will foam and bubble.

3. Now ask an adult to quickly pick up the pitcher, and tilt it carefully over the candle, as if pouring water onto the flame. They must tip it only slightly, so that no liquid or foam gets out.

4. If it works, the candle flame will flicker and go out.

HOW DOES IT WORK?

As you've seen with other experiments in this book, when vinegar and baking soda react together, they make a gas, carbon dioxide. Carbon dioxide is heavier than air, which means you can "pour" it out of a jug and it will flow downward. The candle flame needs oxygen from the air to keep burning. But the carbon dioxide gas pushes the air out of the way, so the candle goes out.

Some types of fire extinguishers contain carbon dioxide gas.

UNBELIEVABLE FORKS

Find out how to make two forks balance in a way that REALLY looks as if it shouldn't be possible. It is possible, though, thanks to the laws of balancing, but it will take a lot of practice to get right.

WHAT YOU'LL NEED:
* Two matching forks (ideally not very precious ones)
* Two cocktail sticks, toothpicks, or similar-length pieces of wooden skewers
* A lot of patience!

1. First, push the two forks together so that their tines (the pointy bits) overlap and line up, like this.

2. Now take one of the sticks and push it through the forks where they overlap. Push the forks inward to jam them onto the stick. Keep the stick as close to the center as possible.

3. Once the stick is jammed in, you should be able to find a point on the stick where it will balance on your finger.

This can be done, but it's tricky, and it may take some time to get the stick in exactly the right place and find the balancing point. Keep trying! If you find it too difficult, ask an adult to see if they can do it.

4. Take the other stick, and hold it point-upward. Now try to balance the stick with the forks on it on the very tip of the point. When you manage it—quick! Get someone to take a photo!

HOW DOES IT WORK?

An object balances on its "center of mass." That means the point that has an equal amount of weight all around it. For example, to balance a simple-shaped object like a plate on your finger, you'd put your finger right in the middle. The forks and toothpick make a much more complicated shape. It looks strange when it's balancing, but the center of mass really is near the end of the stick. That's because the handles of the forks reach back behind the stick, and spread the weight out.

GLOSSARY

airborne When an object is being carried by the air.

calcium carbonate A white, chalky substance found in shells, corals, and many rocks.

carbon dioxide A gas that is colorless and doesn't smell. It is a very small part of the air we breathe.

gravity A force which tries to pull two objects together. Earth's gravity is what keeps us on the ground, and what makes objects fall.

helium A gas that, at room temperature, is lighter than air.

mass The amount of matter a body contains.

particle A tiny piece of matter.

porous Containing a lot of holes.

pressure A force that is placed on an object.

refraction The process of light bouncing off an object and changing its course.

submerge To place something under liquids.

triboluminescence Light caused by rubbing or scratching an object.

FURTHER INFORMATION

Books

Heinecke, Liz Lee. *STEAM Lab For Kids: 52 Creative Hands-On Projects for Exploring Science, Technology, Engineering, Art, and Math.* Beverly, MA: Quarry Books, 2018.

Isaac, Dawn. *101 Brilliant Things For Kids To Do With Science.* London, UK: Kyle Books, 2017.

Mould, Steve. *How To Be A Scientist.* London, UK: DK Children, 2017.

Russell, Harriet. *This Book Thinks You're a Scientist: Imagine, Experiment, Create.* London, UK: Thames and Hudson, 2016.

Tatarsky, Daniel. *Cool Science Tricks: 50 Fantastic Feats For Kids Of All Ages.* London, UK: DK Publishing, 2012.

Websites

http://www.sciencekids.co.nz/experiments.html
A whole host of experiments that let you explore the world of science.

https://youtu.be/OntX1115Tw4
This video shows you how to create bubbles within bubbles!

https://youtu.be/DSCjLR4TCgg
The experiment in this video shows you how to create a flame that travels!

INDEX

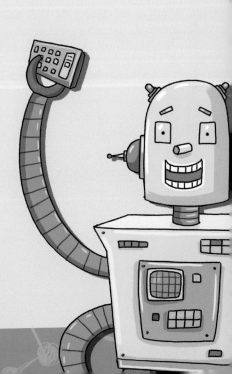